To my two lovelies, Aunt Betty Boop and Uncle Honey Bun —S. B-R.

My deepest thanks to Susan Pearson, the BEST editor in the world,
and to David Slonim, whose delightful illustrations always make me giggle.

. . .

To Jonathan, Daniel, Michael, and Mary —D. S.

Text © 2007 by Sheri Bell-Rehwoldt.
Illustrations © 2007 by David Slonim.

Edited by Susan Pearson.
Book design by Kristine Brogno and David Slonim.
Typeset in Highlander and Slappy.
The illustrations in this book were rendered in oil paint,
pencil, and ball point pen on linen.
Manufactured in China.
ISBN 978-0-8118-5460-3

Library of Congress
Cataloging-in-Publication Data available.

10 9 8 7 6 5 4 3 2

Chronicle Books LLC
680 Second Street, San Francisco, California 94107

www.chroniclekids.com

You Think It's Easy Being the Tooth Fairy?

BY **Sheri Bell-Rehwoldt**   ILLUSTRATED BY **David Slonim**

chronicle books · san francisco

You think it's **easy** being the tooth fairy?
Well, it's not. It takes skill! It takes daring!
Thank goodness I am here to do the job.

Let's get one thing straight, OK?
I **NEVER** wear pink flouncing skirts
or twinkling glass slippers! That's
Cinderella. She does a lot of sitting
around the castle looking pretty.
BORING!
Me, I'm an action kind of gal.
I live for danger!
For suspense!

Let's get clear on another thing, shall we?
I **DON'T** rely on elves to help me out
or flying reindeer to get me around.
That's Santa. You know, the big "Ho-Ho"
in red. Don't get me wrong, he's a
great guy—but all that help has
made him soft.

I'm **TOUGH!**

Check out my muscles!
I got these lugging thousands
of quarters around every night.

And I'm **SMART!** Take my amazing Tooth-o-Finder, for example. I invented it.

Ting! Ting! Ting!

I bet you didn't know that baby teeth come with built-in homing beacons, did you?

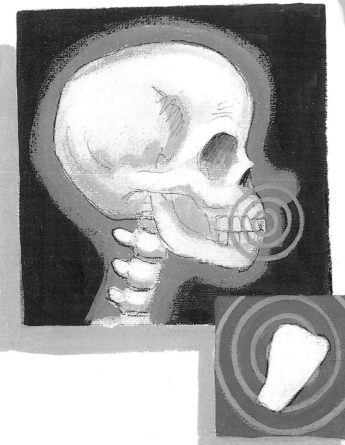

With my trusty Tooth-o-Finder, I can easily locate each tooth's *ting-ting-ting* when it's ready to come out.

After I lock onto your tooth's signal, I use my Spy-o-Binoculars (patent pending) to scope out your house and plan my entry.

Good thing I'm **ATHLETIC!**

Graceful. Poetry in motion.

I bob, I duck, I roll with the punches.

Believe you me, every tooth mission

brings danger—usually on four legs.

Dogs want to chase me.

Gerbils want to flatten me.

Cats want to swat me,
squash me, squeeze me—
even eat me!

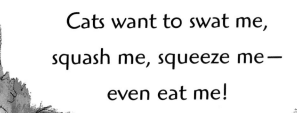

Pets really cut into my work schedule. But so do **YOU!** Sorry, kiddos, but I've got too many teeth on my schedule to play games with you. So I really need you to follow the rules.

DO NOT:

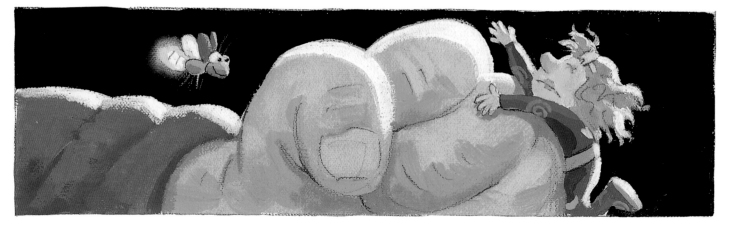

Clutch tooth in sweaty palm.

Hide tooth in pajama pocket.

Wrap tooth in snotty tissue or smelly sock.

DO:

Clean all blood and spit off tooth.

Place tooth carefully beneath lower right-hand corner of pillow.

Sleep soundly. Lie still. Make like a toothbrush.

WONDERFUL! This tooth was right where it should have been—and look how clean it is! Emily gets an A+! And I get another great photo for my scrapbook!

Ting! Ting! Ting!

Eureka! My Tooth-o-Finder's going crazy!

Seven-year-old boy in Honolulu, Hawaii.

Seven-year-old quintuplets in San Antonio, Texas.

Six-year-old girl in Juneau, Alaska.

Wow! This is going to be a LOONNNGGG night!

Whew! All done for tonight! Time for some shut-eye. But never fear, my dears. I'll be ready to fly the second my Tooth-o-Finder starts *ting-ting-ting*ing. I've got my ears peeled for **YOUR** pearly whites!

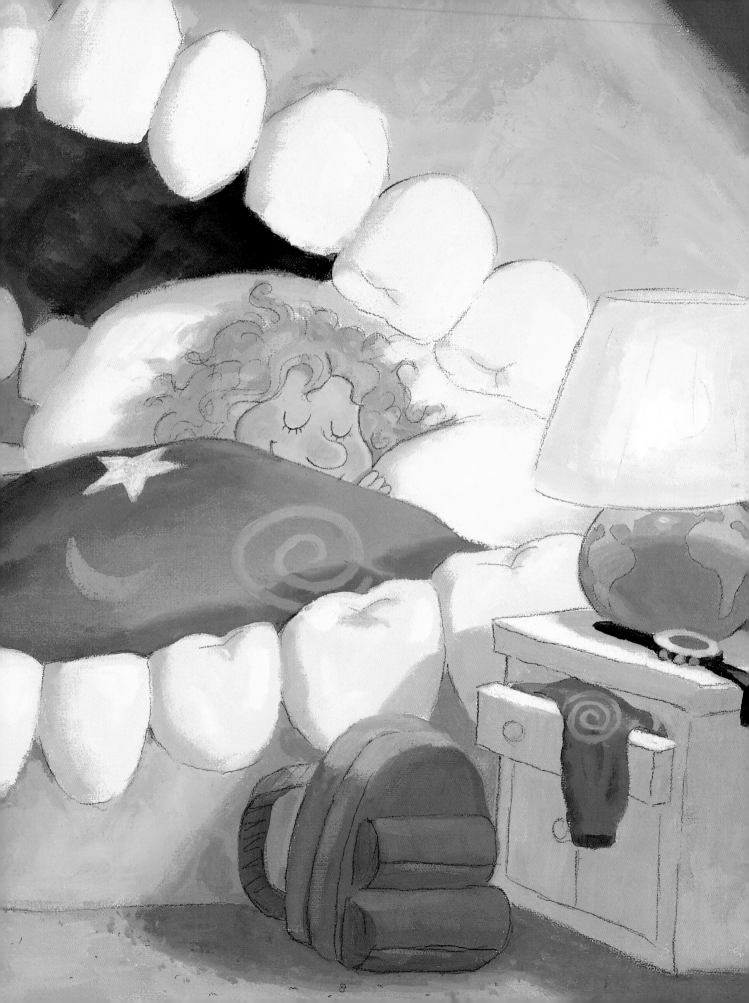

Maria

Gabe

Keisha